# Raimundo
## THE UNWILLING WARRIOR

*by* MARIANA PRIETO

*illustrated by*
BEATRICE DARWIN

HARVEY HOUSE, INC., *Publishers*
Irvington-on-Hudson, New York

Pepe went up the stone steps to Don Fecundo's big, polished front door. As he knocked with the brass knocker, his knees shook. This was an important day for him: He felt in his pocket to make sure that his money was there.

Nearby, peering at him through the fence, stood the object of his visit. He was a small, young rooster. His feathers were the same golden brown as Pepe's smiling face. Pepe had admired him for days. Every morning, as he passed on his way to school, he stopped to talk to the little cock. And the little cock seemed to know him and be his friend.

Now, at last, Don Fecundo opened the heavy wooden door. He looked out, then down at Pepe.

"*Hola,* what do you want, small boy?" he asked in his deep voice. His fat belly shook as he spoke through his bushy mustache.

"Tomorrow is Easter," Pepe said.

"I know," Don Fecundo replied. His thick black eyebrows met in a frown. "Did you knock on my front door and take me away from my domino game to tell me this?"

"Oh, no," Pepe said. "I only wanted to say why I am here. I should like to buy that little cock." He pointed to the rooster peeking through the slats in the fence. "I would like to buy him as an Easter present for myself," he added.

Pepe reached in his pocket and took out some centavos. He held them out in the palm of his hand for Don Fecundo to see.

9

"Buy him!" Don Fecundo shouted. "There is not enough money anywhere to buy him! His ancestors are the finest in all of Spain. From Jerez they come. He will grow to be one of my strongest fighting cocks. He will win me many *pesos* in the *valla* ring."

"Please," Pepe begged "*please* do not put him in the cockfights. He is too timid. He will have his eyes picked out, or his head split. He is different from the other cocks. I know. I watch him every day. And I talk to him from outside the fence when I pass. He likes bird songs, just as I do. He listens as I do. He raises his head and listens when the birds sing. I have seen him."

"Nonsense," Don Fecundo said. "If your friends see you listening to bird's songs, they may call you a sissy or say that you are *estúpido*."

Pepe knew what Don Fecundo meant. He did not like to fight on the playground as other boys did. Nor anywhere else for that matter. He found no fun in hurting people; no fun in making someone's nose bleed.

"No, boy," Don Fecundo said, "I will not sell that fine young cock. His name is Raimundo. His name will be on the banners in front of all the cock-fighting *vallas*. He will be famous. Now I must get back to my domino game." Don Fecundo turned and closed the great door.

Pepe sighed as he moved away. Maybe things would change. He wanted Raimundo very much. He had carefully saved his *centavos* to buy him. Maybe Don Fecundo would sell him for a better price and Pepe could save him from becoming an unwilling warrior.

Pepe's father had died when Pepe was very small. He lived with his mother and grandmother and three sisters, Dolores, Cecilia, and Violeta. Except for Pepe, it was a family of women, and all of them older than he.

None of his sisters shared his interests. The girls talked only of ribbons for their hair or lace for their dresses. His mother talked only of the housework, and of how difficult it was to make a living as a seam-stress. And his grandmother was always busy over the cook stove.

Pepe wanted someone to care about things he cared about. This is why he liked Raimundo. Every day as he passed Don Fecundo's house, the cock was waiting for him.

Pepe would talk to him, and Raimundo would peck at his finger when he stuck it through a space in the fence. This was how Pepe noticed that Raimundo listened when the mockingbirds sang. He stopped pecking one day in order to listen attentively to the bird song.

"You could sing the way they do, I'll bet," Pepe
said to Raimundo. "You are like that bird, only you
are prettier and stronger."

Raimundo looked at Pepe and began to cackle.
Then his tone changed. It sounded as if he were try-
ing to sing.

"Qui-qui-ri-qui," he chanted.

A mockingbird swooped down low over him and
tried to peck him on the head. But Raimundo did not
try to defend himself. He just went on crow-singing.

15

Pepe laughed. He thought about it all the way to school. It would be fun to have a singing cock. His mother had agreed that he could have a rooster for a pet. But he did not want any ordinary rooster from the market. He wanted his friend, Raimundo.

As the months went by the cock grew more sturdy and more handsome. His tail was like an arch of brightly-colored silken ribbons and his feathers glistened in the sunlight, as if they were freshly oiled.

One day when Pepe had stopped to admire Raimundo, Don Fecundo came out to speak to him.

"Today is a big day for Raimundo," he said. "Today he will fight his first fight."

"Oh, no," Pepe whispered. "Please, no, señor."

"Oh, yes, *si, si*. He will fight this afternoon. Last week I held him in front of another cock. Face to face, to *topar* or try him. He wanted to jump out of my hands to get to the other cock. He is light on his feet and quick," Don Fecundo said. There was pride in his voice.

"Yes," he nodded, "this afternoon he will be in the *valla* ring at San Isidro. After he wins there, I will take him later to other rings to fight. He will fight in all the *barrios* of town. I have great plans for him. One day he will be the champion fighting cock of all the world!" He curled the ends of his black mustache between his fingers as he spoke. "He will earn much money for me. And fame."

"I do not think he wants to be a fighter," Pepe said. "You can push him to combat, but his heart will not be in it. He is like a soldier who is forced to fight. I think he has no love of blood." Pepe shook his head. "He is peaceful," he added.

"Such foolishness," Don Fecundo snorted. "You are too serious for a boy of your years. Come on the afternoon of the Rosca de Reyes and watch the fights. You will see betting and money-changing and excitement and you will see for yourself what a fine warrior Raimundo is."

Pepe shook his head sadly as he continued on his way. He did not want to see Raimundo hurt and bleeding. He did not believe that the little cock would fight. Not even to protect himself.

Although he could not bear to think of the fight,
Pepe could not stay away from it. So, on the day of
the Rosca celebration he went to *La Valla de San
Isidro*. It was hot and dusty inside. Many men wear-
ing big straw sombreros crowded around the ring.

They shouted for their favorite fighters. They
called their bets to one another and argued who would
win. Some held their fighting cocks in their hands and
smoothed their feathers.

23

At last Pepe saw Don Fecundo arrive with Raimundo in his bag. Each fighting cock was brought in a pillowcase-like bag by his owner. It was time for the first fight to start. The men crowded around the dirt enclosure. A low wooden fence about two feet high kept the fighting cocks inside. The watchers leaned forward anxiously to see.

Pepe got down on his hands and knees so that he could look between the long legs of a man standing in front of him.

Nearby, the owner of a prize cock readied him for the fight. He held the cock in one hand. Then he lifted a bottle of the strong alcohol *aguardiente* drink to his lips. He filled his mouth with it until his cheeks puffed out. Carefully, still holding the cock in his hand, he pushed its feathers back with his other hand. Then he spit the *aguardiente* all over the cock, spraying him with it so that it wet his skin. The cock reacted angrily.

"This will make you fight with fury. This will give you energy," the man said. Then he placed the cock in the ring where his opponent waited.

The men who were watching screamed encouragement.

"*Pícalo!* Peck him. Get him!"

They clapped their hands.

They stomped the earth.

Pepe could stand no more. He could not bear to think what would happen when Raimundo's turn came. He got up from his hands and knees and started toward home.

Mama and Pepe's grandmother and his sisters were waiting for him to cut the traditional Rosca cake that usually held a prize in each piece. The prize might be a ring or a coin. It might be a religious medal, or it might be anything that Grandmother chose to place there when she baked it.

Usually Pepe looked forward to such treats, but today his steps were slow as he entered his house. His heart was heavy as he thought about Raimundo, who wanted to sing rather than fight.

"Que pasa?" Pepe's mother asked. "What is the matter? Come, we are all at the table waiting for you. The *Rosca* is ready for cutting." Mama wore her fiesta dress and looked very happy.

Pepe sat down at the table beside his eldest sister, Rosita. Grandmother was at the head of the table, her place of honor. She sat very erect. Slowly, like a queen giving gifts to her subjects, she cut the cake and placed a piece on each plate.

At last Pepe got his share. He lifted the slice to his mouth and bit down on it. His teeth came down on something hard — so hard that it made a scraping sound. He took the cake from his mouth and broke the slice open. A shining silver peso dropped out! He looked at it. Then he knew what he must do.

"*Gracias,* thank you, dear Grandmother," he said. "Please may I be excused?" He got up from the table. "There is something I must do at once."

Without waiting for a reply from his grandmother or his astonished family, he ran out of the house.

Down the road he ran. He must get to the cockfight before Raimundo was put in the ring. A whole silver peso was a lot more money than he had been able to offer Don Fecundo before. Maybe now Don Fecundo would sell Raimundo.

The way to the *valla* arena was a long one. The afternoon sun was hot and Pepe felt the sweat rolling down his cheeks as he ran. The dust came up to choke him, but he kept going. He must get there before poor Raimundo was put to combat and hurt, or maybe even killed.

When he reached the fight ring, he was so breathless that he could hardly speak.

"Where is Don Fecundo?" he asked an old man.

"I do not know." The man turned toward the ring and paid no attention to Pepe.

The crowd was shouting and screaming, *"Pica, Pica!"*

Raimundo might be in the ring now being pecked. Pepe was not able to see who the fighters were.

At last he edged around to the place where the owner of the *valla* ring stood.

"Where is Don Fecundo," he asked, trembling, "where?"

"He has gone home," the man said quickly, as he reached into a bag at his side and lifted out a brightly-colored cock. Pepe turned away. He felt sick all over. What had happened to Raimundo? And why had Don Fecundo left so early?

Many questions filled his mind as later he walked up the stone steps to Don Fecundo's door. He must know the answers.

Once more he reached for the brass knocker as he had done before. Then, waiting, he turned and saw Raimundo behind the fence, his head sticking through the slats. Pepe's face broke into a wide smile. When Raimundo saw him, he began to crow his happiest cackle.

Don Fecundo opened the great door.

"What do you want now?" he snapped.

"Don Fecundo, señor, I have come with more money." I see Raimundo is well. Perhaps you will sell him to me now that I can offer you more."

"Sell him!" Don Fecundo thundered. "You still want to buy him?"

Pepe nodded. "But *si,* yes, yes, please."

"Take him." Don Fecundo's face flushed with rage. "Take him and get him out of my sight forever. He has made everyone laugh at me. He would not fight. When I put him in the *valla* ring with the other cock, he walked away. He tried to jump over the fence, out of the ring. This one made a fool of me. I am ruined. I, Don Fecundo, the breeder of the finest fighting cocks in all the land."

"Oh," Pepe said, "I knew that he was a smart cock."

"Smart cock, indeed," Don Fecundo growled. "I was going to give him to the cook to make stew of him. But he is so stupid I am sure his meat would be tough. He is not fit to be cooked. Take him, and get out."

"Please," Pepe said, "do not be angry with him — or with me. It's just that we are different." His excitement made his eyes sparkle like dark glass bubbles.

"Get him and go." Don Fecundo pointed to Raimundo.

And so Pepe took Raimundo home. He still had his silver peso that would buy food for his new pet. As he walked down the road carrying Raimundo under his arm, he felt the soft warmth of him.

No longer now would he, Pepe, be the only male in a household of females. Together Raimundo and he would walk in the fields. Together they would listen to the birds sing. At night Raimundo would perch on the footboard of his bed. And early in the morning he would wake Pepe with his crowing.

This Raimundo did the next morning, and for all the mornings thereafter. He "crow-sang" to his young master his own special kind of crow song that no other cock could sing.

45